Three *More* Stories
You Can Read
to Your Dog

Sara Swan Miller
Illustrated by True Kelley

Houghton Mifflin Company
Boston 2000

For Marty, again!
−S. S. M.

For my daughter Jada Lindblom,
and in memory of Pigzy
−T. K.

Text copyright © 2000 by Sara Swan Miller
Illustrations copyright © 2000 by True Kelley

The text of this book is set in 16-point Baskerville Book.
The illustrations are ink and watercolor.

Library of Congress Cataloging-in-Publication Data

Miller, Sara Swan.
Three more stories you can read to your dog / Sara Swan Miller ;
illustrated by True Kelley.
p.   cm.
Summary: Stories addressed to dogs and written from a dog's point
of view, featuring such topics as going to the vet, making friends with
a rocklike creature, and getting a bath.
ISBN 0-395-92293-3
[1. Dogs−Fiction.]   I. Kelley, True, ill.   II. Title.
PZ7.M63344Th   2000
[Fic]−dc21   99-39880   CIP

Printed in Singapore
TWP 10 9 8 7 6 5 4 3 2 1

Contents

Introduction

Is your dog sleeping a lot? Do you know why? Your dog must be feeling bored. You can always read a good book when you have nothing to do. But most dogs never do learn to read, even smart ones like yours.

Your dog needs to hear some stories. Listening to stories is a great way to keep from being bored! Here are three your dog will like.

Always remember to pet your dog while you read. Dogs like that, too.

Come here, you good dog! Look what we have!
More stories for you! Sit down, now. Here is the
first one.

1

The Vet

ONE DAY your friend said, "Come on, good dog, let's go to the doc!"
"Walk?" you said. "Walk! Oh, WOW!"
You jumped up and down and up and down.
You ran around and around and around. Walks are your favorite thing in the world!
Your friend put on your leash. You raced out the door.

"Come here, silly dog," said your friend. "Come get in the car."

"Car?" you said to yourself. "How do you go for a walk in a car?"

Oh well, a drive was almost as much fun as a walk. You jumped into the car.

The drive was great! You hung your head out of
the window. You sniffed and sniffed all the good
smells. You barked at the burglars walking along
the road. You could ride in the car for the rest of
your life!

All at once, the car stopped.
"Here we are!" said your friend.

Wait! You knew this place! It was the vet's house!
Your friend had tricked you!
You hid under the seat. But your friend found you.
You tried hiding behind a tire. But your friend
found you again.
You dug in your heels. But your friend was stronger
than you thought.

The next thing you knew, you were inside!
"This is awful!" you said to yourself. "I am NOT
staying HERE!"
You clawed and clawed at the door. You jumped
and jumped at the window. You smeared nose
juice on the glass. But none of it helped one bit.

Oh, no! Here came the vet!

He lifted you up on a high, slippery table. It was
scary up there! Then he did all kinds of terrible
things.

He poked in your ears. He looked up your nose.
He shined a light in your eyes. He prodded at
your belly. Then he poked around in your mouth.

"Maybe I will bite this nosy vet!" you said to
yourself. "But what if that makes him mad?
Maybe he will do worse things!"

You shed hair all over
his table instead.

Finally the vet was done. He started
poking around on his desk.
"Whew!" you said to yourself.

All at once, OWWWWW! A bee stung you on your back! You whirled around to snap at it. You whirled around and around and around. But the sneaky bee was gone.

"This is awful!" you said to yourself. "First all that poking, and now he keeps bees in his house!"

The vet lifted you down from the table.

"Here, good dog!" he said. "Do you want a biscuit?"

You sniffed at the biscuit. It smelled safe enough. You snapped it up and ran into a corner to eat it.

"But listen, you vet," you muttered, "don't think any old biscuit is going to make me be your friend!"

Then the vet opened the door. Free at last! You raced for the car and leaped inside.

"Now we can go for a real walk!" you said to yourself. But all that poking and prodding and bee-stinging made you tired. You were too tired for a walk. You were too tired even to look out the window. You stretched out on the back seat and slept all the way home.

Hey, good dog, are you ready for another story?
Here is another one just for you.

2

The Strange Rock

ANOTHER TIME, you were having a pokey
day. You were done digging in the garden. You
were tired of chewing on sticks. You had barked
at the neighbors enough for one day. What was
there left to do?

"I know!" you said to yourself. "I will ask my
friend to play ball with me!"

Your friend was sitting under a tree.

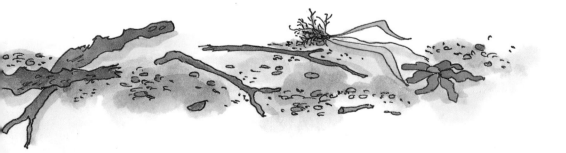

"Ball!" you said. "Ball! Ball!"

"Go away, dog," said your friend. "I am busy reading a book."

You sat down and wagged your tail. Maybe your friend would read you a story! You loved stories! You wagged your tail some more. But your friend did not even look up.

"Hmph!" you said to yourself. "My friend is no fun anymore."

You went off to find your favorite tree. You lay
down and closed your eyes for a nap. There was
nothing else to do.

Then you heard something odd.

Rustle, rustle, scrape, scrape. Someone was
coming through the woods! You ran to find out
who it was.

A rock was walking through the leaves!
"What a strange rock," you said to yourself. "A
rock with feet! And a head! And a tail!"
Maybe the rock wanted to play. Maybe the rock
would be your new friend! You ran up to the rock.
"BARK! BARK!" you said to the rock. "BARK
BARK ARK ARK
ARK ARK ARK!"

But the rock did not want to play. It pulled its head and its tail and its feet inside. It just sat there.

"Come out, rock!" you said. "Play with me!"

But the rock did not come out. Maybe the rock was shy. Maybe you should have asked it more quietly.

"Whuff! Whuff!" you said. "Whuff whuff whuff whuff whuff whuff."

But the rock just sat.

Then you had a good idea. You would bring it something to play with! You ran off to find your ball. You bounced it off the rock.

"Come out, rock!" you said. "I want to play with you!"

The rock did not move.

"Maybe rocks do not like balls," you said to
yourself. "Maybe they like sticks better."
You ran to find a stick. You dropped it in front
of the rock.

"Come out, rock!" you said. "Please?"
The rock said nothing. It did nothing. It just sat
there. Your new friend was not much fun after all.
"Maybe rocks cannot see very well," you said to
yourself. "Maybe they like squeaky toys better."

You went hunting for your squeaky toy. You looked under the porch. No squeaky toy.

You looked under the car. No squeaky toy. You nosed around under your tree. Still no squeaky toy. You searched everywhere.

There it was! It was hiding in a flower bed! You snatched it up and ran back to the rock.

Where was the rock? It had vanished! Poof! Just like that!

"That rock was more than strange," you said to yourself. "That rock was magic!"

But now you did not have a new friend anymore. Not even a boring new friend.

Wait, here came your old friend!

"Hey, good dog," said your old friend. "Do you want to play?"

"What a silly question!" you said to yourself. You and your friend had a great time! You played Fetch the Stick. You played Catch the Ball. You played Hide the Squeaky Toy. Finally, you were all played out. You stood in the hot sun and panted.

"Enough!" you said.
"Enough!"

All that playing made you sleepy. It was hard
work making your friend happy. You crept off
and lay down under your tree.
"I am so glad I still have my old friend," you
said to yourself. "Old friends are the best!"
You curled up in the shade and went to sleep.

Why are you wagging your tail, good dog? Do you want to hear another story? All right, here is the last one.

3

The Bath

ONE MORNING, you were taking a nap on the couch. All of a sudden you woke up. You had a horrible itch behind your ear! You scratched it and scratched it. Oh, no! There was another itch on your shoulder! You scratched it, too.

There was another itch! And another! And another! You had itches all over! You scratched and scratched and scratched. Then you scratched some more.

Oh, good! Your friend was coming to help you scratch!

"Uh-oh," said your friend. "You must have fleas."
Your friend went away.

"Some friend!" you said to yourself. "Now I have to do all this scratching by myself."

You scratched and scratched and scratched and
scratched. Then you heard an awful sound. Water
was running in the bathtub!
"No fair!" you said to yourself. "I have enough
trouble right now! Not a bath, too!"

Your friend was so mean! You hid behind the couch.
Then you went back to work on your itches.

"Come on out from behind that couch, silly dog,"
said your friend. "You need a bath."

You did NOT need a bath! You shot out from
behind the couch. You ran through the living
room. You raced through the kitchen. Your
friend raced after you.

You ran upstairs.
You ran downstairs.
Your friend was still after you!

You ran back upstairs.
You dashed into a closet.
"No one will ever find me here!"
you panted.

"What are you doing in the closet?" said your friend.
"Come have your bath now, silly dog." Your friend
grabbed your collar and pulled you to the bathroom.

"Jump in!" said your so-called friend. Oh well, you might as well get it over with. You jumped into the bath.

Your friend sprayed water at you. You had water in your ears and water in your eyes. You even got water in your mouth.

"I hate this part!" you said to yourself.

Then your friend poured something on your back. Your friend started to rub you all over.

"Ahhh," you said to yourself. "Now this part is not so bad!"
Your friend rubbed and rubbed. It felt wonderful!
But then your friend started spraying water at you again. It was horrible!

"Phooey!" you said to yourself. "I wish my friend would go back to the good part."

Finally, your friend was done. You leaped out of the awful tub. You started to shake that nasty water out of your fur.

"No, no!" said your friend.
"Let me dry you!"

Your friend bundled you up in a towel and rubbed you and rubbed you.

"Mmmmm," you said to yourself. "I forgot how nice this part is!"

"Okay," said your friend. "All done!"

Yay! You were free! You ran back to your couch.
You needed to get back to work on your itches.

"Huh!" you said to yourself. "Where did all those
itches go?"
It was funny. The itches were gone! They must
have fallen off when you were running away from
the bath!

"I am one speedy dog," you said to yourself. "I am faster than itches!" Now you could get back to your nap in peace. You curled up on the couch and went back to sleep.